anada's
AND & PEOPLE

NEW BRUNSWICK

Leah Sarich

Weigl

CALGARY

www.weigl.com

Published by Weigl Educational Publishers Limited
6325 10 Street SE
Calgary, Alberta   T2H 2Z9

Website: www.weigl.com
Copyright ©2008 WEIGL PUBLISHERS INC.

Library and Archives Canada Cataloguing in Publication

Sarich, Leah
        New Brunswick / Leah Sarich.

(Canada's land and people)
Includes index.
ISBN 978-1-55388-371-5 (bound)
ISBN 978-1-55388-372-2 (pbk.)

        1. New Brunswick--Juvenile literature. I. Title. II. Series.
FC2461.2.S275 2007   j971.5'1   C2007-902233-2

Printed in the United States of America
1 2 3 4 5 6 7 8 9 0 11 10 09 08 07

We acknowledge the financial support of the Government of Canada through the Book Publishing Industry Development Program (BPIDP) for our publishing activities.

Photograph credits: Friends of Beaubears Island: page 21 top; New Brunswick Sports Hall of Fame: page 19 bottom; Provincial Government of New Brunswick: page 3 bottom, 4 bottom, 11 top right; 12, 13 bottom, 14, 15 top, 15 middle right, 15 middle left, 15 bottom, 17 middle right, 20 top; UNB Media Production: page 17 middle left.

Project Coordinator
Heather C. Hudak

Design
Terry Paulhus

Contents

About New Brunswick

New Brunswick ranks eighth in size among Canada's provinces. Trees cover most of the province's 72,908 square kilometres of land.

Water borders at least three sides of Canada's three Maritime Provinces. New Brunswick is the largest of the Maritime Provinces, followed by Nova Scotia and Prince Edward Island.

New Brunswick joined Confederation on July 1, 1867. The province's name honours King George I and the royal family of Brunswick-Lüneberg.

The province's official **tartan** celebrates New Brunswick's Scottish heritage. Five colours on the tartan have special meanings. Dark green is a symbol of the province's trees. Light green honours farming. Red shows the loyalty of early **Loyalists**. Blue celebrates the province's location near the sea. Gold highlights its potential wealth.

ABOUT THE FLAG

New Brunswick's flag became official in 1965. The gold lion on a red field reflects the province's British ties. The boat on the sea shows New Brunswick's seaside location and its shipbuilding history.

LEGEND

Yukon

Northwest Territories

Nunavut

British Columbia

Alberta

Manitoba

Saskatchewan

Ontario

Quebec

Newfoundland & Labrador

Prince Edward Island

New Brunswick

Nova Scotia

N

ACTION Make a tartan to show what is special about where you live. Use different coloured paper strips. You might use green for fields or white for clean air. Glue two strips lengthwise on a piece of paper. Leave about 3 centimetres between them. Then, glue two strips across over the first two strips. Leave 3 centimetres between them. It should look a bit like a tic-tac-toe board when you are done.

Places to Visit in New Brunswick

New Brunswick offers many special places to visit and exciting things to do. This map shows just a few ideas. Where would you like to visit in New Brunswick? Can you find these places on the map?

The ocean is less than 200 kilometres from any place in New Brunswick. Summer tourists flock to the sandy beaches along the Gulf of St. Lawrence.

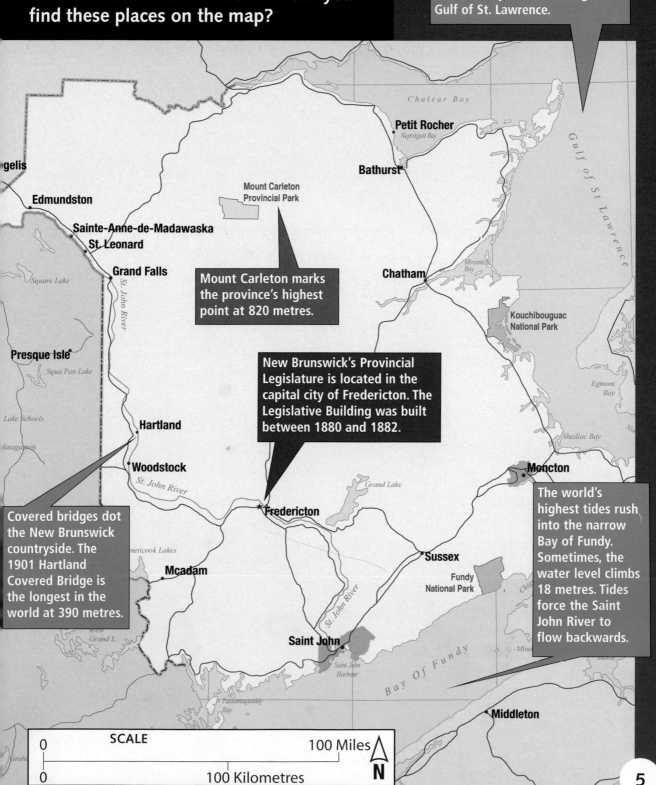

Mount Carleton marks the province's highest point at 820 metres.

New Brunswick's Provincial Legislature is located in the capital city of Fredericton. The Legislative Building was built between 1880 and 1882.

Covered bridges dot the New Brunswick countryside. The 1901 Hartland Covered Bridge is the longest in the world at 390 metres.

The world's highest tides rush into the narrow Bay of Fundy. Sometimes, the water level climbs 18 metres. Tides force the Saint John River to flow backwards.

SCALE
0   100 Miles
0   100 Kilometres
N

Beautiful Landscapes

Glaciers scraped across New Brunswick more than 10,000 years ago. They left behind beautiful landscapes, from craggy mountains to rolling meadows and rocky coastlines. Streams, rivers, and lakes sparkle beneath tall forests. Across New Brunswick, temperatures range from about –9 degrees Celsius in the winter to 19 degrees Celsius in the summer.

Mountains in the **Appalachian Range** crown northwestern New Brunswick. The Saint John River starts there and stretches 673 kilometres across the province.

Thick forests cover the hills rolling across New Brunswick's centre region. Wood pulp is one of the province's important products. The province produces about $1.5 billion worth of wood pulp each year.

Rugged and steep terrain cuts through the Caledonia Highlands and Kent Hills in the south. Then, the land drops to tidal marshes and the sea.

Grassy plains slope toward the eastern coast. Families can explore the sand dunes, calm shores, and wind-swept beaches there.

Fur, Feathers, and Flowers

Wildlife thrives in New Brunswick, especially in the large forests that cover most of the land. Moose, mink, fox, white-tailed deer, rabbits, and other animals live in the forests. Evergreens are most common in the North. Maple and birch trees mix among the pine trees in other parts of the province. Wild berries and other plants feed many animals and birds.

New Brunswick chose the purple violet for its official flower in 1936. People use the dainty flowers for jam, syrup, and medicine.

Hundreds of birds live in New Brunswick. The black-capped chickadee was named the province's official bird in 1983.

At least 12 different species of whales pass by New Brunswick every year looking for food. Most whales eat **krill**, fish, and squid. The 25-metre blue whale can eat up to 3.6 metric tonnes of food each day. It is the planet's largest mammal.

In 1987, New Brunswick made the balsam fir its official tree. Balsam firs are popular for Christmas trees because they stay green indoors for a long time.

Fiddlehead ferns grow in New Brunswick's swampy woodlands. People pick them in the spring for food.

Rich in Resources

New Brunswick has more woodland than any other province. Its trees provide homes for wildlife and places for people to hike, camp, and play. The forestry industry provides jobs for more than 16,000 people. Workers harvest trees and make lumber, pulp, and paper. New Brunswick is also rich with minerals in the earth and fish in the sea.

New Brunswick is Canada's leading producer of zinc, lead, **bismuth**, and **antimony**. At the Mining and Mineral Interpretation Centre in Petit-Rocher, visitors can see what it is like to travel down a mining shaft. Nearby, the world's largest underground zinc mine operates at Bathurst. This mine has produced about 3.6 million tonnes of zinc, lead, copper, and silver ore each year since 1964.

Tourism has become important to New Brunswick's economy. The province welcomes more than 1.5 million visitors each year. Visitors enjoy festivals, sightseeing, and four seasons of outdoor activities.

New Brunswick fishers harvest lobster mainly in the spring and in December from the cold Atlantic waters. The province produces salmon, trout, and shellfish through **aquaculture**, or water farming.

New Brunswick's main cash crop comes from about 400 potato farmers. Today, New Brunswick sells its potatoes to about 35 countries.

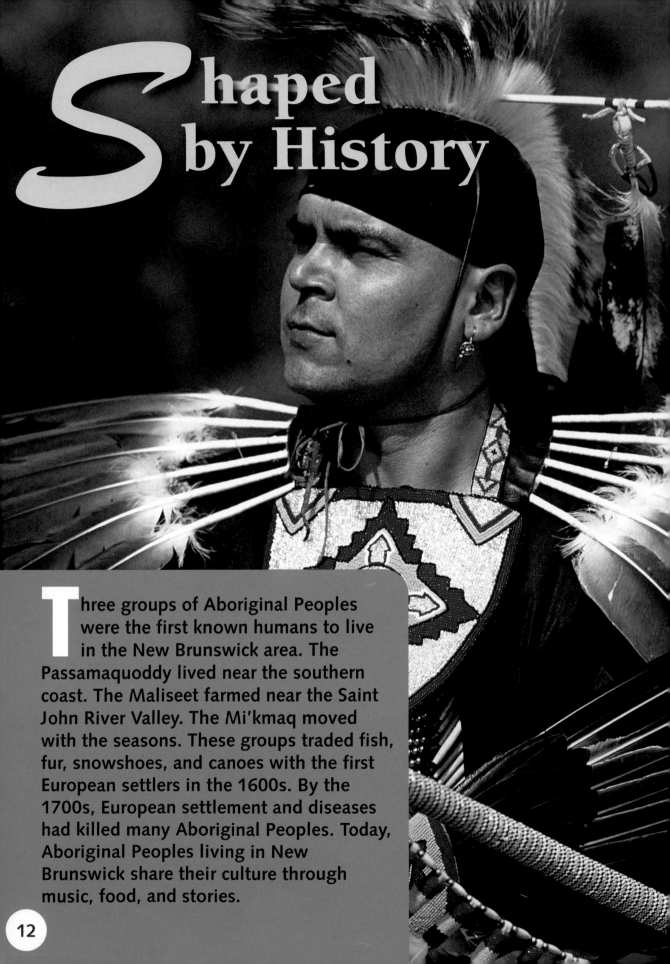

Shaped by History

There groups of Aboriginal Peoples were the first known humans to live in the New Brunswick area. The Passamaquoddy lived near the southern coast. The Maliseet farmed near the Saint John River Valley. The Mi'kmaq moved with the seasons. These groups traded fish, fur, snowshoes, and canoes with the first European settlers in the 1600s. By the 1700s, European settlement and diseases had killed many Aboriginal Peoples. Today, Aboriginal Peoples living in New Brunswick share their culture through music, food, and stories.

Jacques Cartier sailed along New Brunswick's northern coast in 1534. He claimed the land for France. By the late 1600s, French people had settled the Atlantic area. They called it "Acadia." The name means "a place of great natural beauty."

Acadia's timber attracted British settlers in the 1600s. Great Britain and France fought over the land. France lost in 1713. Great Britain drove the Acadians out in 1755. Some escaped to the area near Chaleur Bay. In

1847, Henry Wadsworth Longfellow wrote a long poem called *Evangeline* about the Acadian troubles. Acadians helped keep the French language and traditions alive in Canada. Today, New Brunswick is the only province with both French and English as official languages.

Great Britain lost its American colonies in 1783. Many American settlers still felt loyal to the crown. They fled to the Saint John River Valley, part of Nova Scotia then. Their new settlement quickly grew. In 1784, it became a separate colony called New Brunswick. Its nickname was "The Loyalist Province."

Art and Culture

The province celebrates New Brunswick Day in August and honours its vivid cultural heritage all year long. First Nations, Loyalists, Acadians, Irish, Scots, Danes, and Germans host festivals. Museums across the province showcase history, nature, and art. At an Acadian Historic Village, visitors learn how people once lived in New Brunswick. Theatre and musical performances and many kinds of written works reveal a lively arts community.

The *Village Historique Acadien*, or Acadian Historic Village, at Caraquet, and Kings Landing Historical Settlement near Fredericton feature actors dressed in historic styles.

The Village of Gagetown has been called "one of the ten prettiest towns in Canada." Artists gather here to paint. Many galleries feature their work.

Since 1957, the Miramichi Folksong Festival in Miramichi has featured traditional singers, dancers, fiddlers, and other musicians. Festivals elsewhere for baroque, jazz, and popular music draw large crowds.

Tartan Day is April 6 each year. It honours New Brunswick's strong Scottish heritage. In the summer, the New Brunswick Highland Games and Scottish Festival presents bagpipers, dancers, and other traditional entertainment.

Points of Interest

New Brunswick's natural wonders and scenic beauty offer many places to see in all four seasons. Fundy National Park and Kouchibouguac National Park protect important **habitats**. New Brunswick's oldest mainland lighthouse, dating from 1848, is located at Cape Enrage. Friendly riverfront villages, historic harbour towns, and bustling cities welcome visitors. Festivals invite people to sample delicious **ethnic** foods and shop for handmade crafts.

Powerful tides in the Bay of Fundy grind away **sandstone** from the ocean floor. Trees and grass grow above the waterline on the Hopewell Rocks. At low tide, they look like huge flowerpots.

Grand Falls is near the United States border. Here, the Saint John River tumbles 23 metres into a rocky **gorge**. Swirling currents from spring thaws have worn deep wells into the gorge floor. Some wells measure 9 metres deep. Dry summer weather lets hikers climb down 250 steps to see the wells.

Founded in 1785, the University of New Brunswick has several **campus** locations today. It is North America's first public university. It is Canada's oldest English-speaking university.

New Brunswick's second-largest city is Moncton. People call Moncton the "Hub City" because of its location at the centre of the Maritime Provinces.

Sports and Activities

New Brunswick's wilderness calls to adventurers. They camp, fish, hike, bike, snowshoe, ski, and snowmobile in this outdoor wonderland. New Brunswick does not host any major-league sports teams. However, athletes from the province have competed internationally in sports such as hockey, speed skating, boxing, curling, basketball, baseball, and rhythmic gymnastics. Many schools and local recreation centres encourage **amateur** athletes in almost all sports.

The Saint John Sea Dogs hockey team competes in "The Q," the Quebec Major Junior Hockey League. Players are 20 years old or younger. They go to school in the morning and practise in the afternoon.

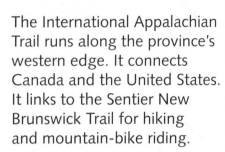

Miramichi's salmon stream attracts fishers each spring. The river waters near Woodstock fill with smallmouth bass every year.

The International Appalachian Trail runs along the province's western edge. It connects Canada and the United States. It links to the Sentier New Brunswick Trail for hiking and mountain-bike riding.

In Fredericton, the New Brunswick Sports Hall of Fame honours the province's star athletes and teams. It includes sports such as basketball, hockey, curling, boxing, rowing, baseball, golf, and rugby.

*W*hat Others Are Saying

Many people have great things to say about New Brunswick.

"The St. John is a fine river equal in magnitude to the Connecticut or Hudson, with a fine harbour at the mouth, accessible at all seasons of the year, never frozen or obstructed by ice."

"New Brunswick is a place where you'll discover the highest tides in the world, where rivers are bountiful and inspirational and bays win beauty pageants. You will be fascinated by the fragile beauty of coastal dunes and inspired by the Appalachians, some of the oldest mountains on the planet."

"Through thousands of years and many cultures, the [Beaubears] island has stood like a sentinel, marking history in cruel and kind ways. Slicing the mighty Miramichi River into two branches it served as a centuries-old Mi'kmaq meeting ground for trade and stories of the hunt. The Natives who knew the island well called it *Quoomeneegook* (pine island)."

"New Brunswick's varied landscape, coastal setting and charming, small-town atmosphere makes it a traveller's delight."

ACTION Think about the place where you live. Come up with some words to describe your province, city, or community. Are there rolling hills and deep valleys? Can you see trees or lakes? What are some of the features of the land, people, and buildings that make your home special? Use these words to write a paragraph about the place where you live.

Test Your Knowledge

What have you learned about New Brunswick?
Try answering the following questions.

1 Where is the Fundy National Park located? What is special about the sea there?

2 What did First Nations peoples trade with Europeans in the 1600s? Visit the library to learn more about how European settlers changed the ways First Nations peoples lived in the 1600s.

3 What types of birds live in New Brunswick? Look online to learn more about New Brunswick's birds and their habitats. Write a paragraph about your favourite New Brunswick bird and draw a picture of it.

Create Your Own Emblem

Choose three important things found in New Brunswick. For example, you might choose the official bird, the official tree, and Aboriginal canoes. Make an official emblem that shows the three items you selected. Write a paragraph about why you chose these things. Explain what they mean to people who live in New Brunswick.

Further Research

Books

To find out more about New Brunswick and other Canadian provinces and territories, visit your local library. Most libraries have computers that connect to a database for researching information. If you input a key word, you will be provided with a list of books in the library that contain information on that topic. Non-fiction books are arranged numerically, using their call number. Fiction books are organized alphabetically by the author's last name.

Websites

The World Wide Web is a good source of information. Reliable websites usually include government sites, educational sites, and online encyclopedias. Visit the following sites to learn more about New Brunswick.

Go to the Government of New Brunswick's website to learn about the province's government, history, and climate.
www.gnb.ca/index-e.asp

Visit Tourism New Brunswick, a travel site, to learn more about things to do and see in the province.
www.tourismnewbrunswick.ca/en-ca/

For fun facts, photos of New Brunswick and activities for kids, visit the Kidzone.
www.kidzone.ws/geography/newbrunswick

Glossary

amateur: to play for fun, not pay

antimony: a flaky and toxic metal used in batteries, paints, and flame-proofing materials

Appalachian Range: a line of mountains stretching from Quebec to the Gulf of Mexico in eastern North America

aquaculture: the farming of plants and animals that live in water; also called "fish-farming" or "ocean ranching"

bismuth: a reddish-grey metal

campus: the area where buildings for a school, hospital, or other organization are located

ethnic: refers to the customs, food, and traditions of different groups of people from all over the world

glaciers: slow-moving ice masses

gorge: a steep valley, often with a river running through it

habitats: the places where plants or animals normally live in nature

krill: shrimp-like crustaceans that live in large schools

Loyalists: people who were loyal to the British government

sandstone: rock made of pressed sand-sized grains

tartan: a fabric woven in a plaid pattern, usually with colours and designs that have special meanings

Index